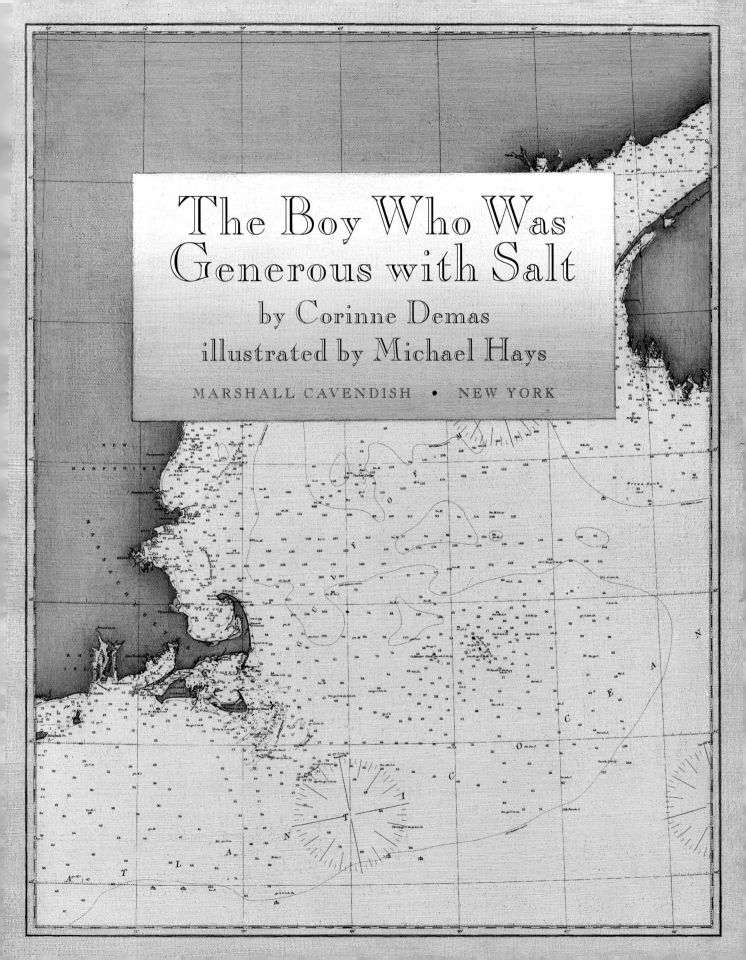

The Boy Who Was Generous with Salt

by Corinne Demas

illustrated by Michael Hays

MARSHALL CAVENDISH • NEW YORK

ACKNOWLEDGEMENTS

The author and illustrator wish to thank the Wellfleet Historical Society; Philip L. Budlong, Associate
Curator, Mystic Seaport; Andrew W. German, Fisheries Expert, Mystic Seaport; Bonnie M. Snow,
Historian, Orleans Historical Society; Nancy Vivante; and Elaine Lasker vonBruns.
Nautical charts provided by the Historical Map and Chart Collection, Office of Coast Survey/NOAA

Marshall Cavendish, 99 White Plains Road, Tarrytown, NY 10591
Text copyright © 2002 by Corinne Demas Illustrations copyright © 2002 by Michael Hays

Library of Congress Cataloging-in-Publication Data
Demas, Corinne.
The boy who was generous with salt / by Corinne Demas; illustrated by Michael Hays.   p.   cm.
Summary: Having gone to sea as a cook on a nineteenth-century fishing schooner, Ned thinks that
if he uses up all the salt on board he will get to return home in time for his ninth birthday.
ISBN 0-7614-5099-8
[1. Cooks—Fiction. 2. Birthdays—Fiction. 3. Sea stories.] I. Hays, Michael, date, ill. II. Title.
PZ7.D39145 Bo2001   [Fic]—dc21   99-055535

The illustrations are painted in acrylics on gessoed linen canvas.
The text is set in 14 point Goudy Old Style.
Printed in Hong Kong
First edition
6 5 4 3 2 1

For my son, Austin—C. D.

For Christa—M.H.

Ned was not yet nine when he went to sea as a cook on the fishing schooner

Adeline

His mother had taught him how to make biscuits and chowder and sweet cake. She packed all his things in a calico pillowcase.

His little sister Nancy gave him a cloth bag filled with lavender from the garden.

"That's so you can smell home when you're far out at sea," she said.

❀

She cried and hugged him when he left.

"You'll be back by your birthday, won't you Neddy?" she asked.

"I hope so!" said Ned. It was now the end of March. He'd be nine at the end of July, and by then they should have their catch. He wished he didn't have to go, but his family needed the money he would earn, and he was lucky to get a place on a fishing boat this season.

He kissed them all goodbye: Nancy, his mother, his little brothers, Sam and Thomas, even their dog and the cat and the cow. He slung his bedsack and his pillowcase on his shoulders and set off for Wellfleet Harbor. He looked back and waved until the little house was out of sight.

Hays © 2002

The *Adeline* was all packed up with provisions for the trip. There were barrels of beans and barrels of dried beef and barrels of rice and flour and corn meal. There was a big barrel of molasses to sweeten the coffee, since sugar was too dear. There were fifty barrels of water to last all the months at sea, and barrels of salt for the cod they'd catch.

The captain was a cousin of Ned's father, who had died some years before. He showed Ned his berth below and where to stow his gear. Ned watched from the deck as Wellfleet, then Cape Cod, disappeared in the distance.

ᔕᔕᔕᔕ

The first two days at sea Ned was so seasick he could barely stand. The men all teased him, especially the first mate, Ezra. Ezra had eyes that didn't line up right and only a few teeth left in his mouth. "You have the makings of a captain, I can see," he joked.

It took nearly two weeks to reach the Grand Banks, the best fishing ground. The captain chose a spot to anchor, and they took in the sails and threw out the fishing lines. Land was so far away it was hard to believe it was still there at all.

Every morning Ned got up at three to start the fire in the wood stove and make biscuits and coffee for breakfast for the crew. Every day he made dinner and supper. After every meal he washed up with soap and salt water, and scoured the tin plates with ashes from the stove.

At night there were no lights in the distance, only stars. In his bunk Ned pressed his face against the lavender Nancy had given him. Only the sea could hear him cry.

"When will we be going back home, Sir?" Ned asked the captain.

"When we've wet our salt," the captain said. "That means when all the salt's used up."

"When will we wet our salt?" Ned asked.

"Maybe by November," Ezra said, and all the men laughed.

"You in some hurry to get back to shore, lad?" the captain asked.

"I'd hoped to be home by July 25th, my birthday, sir," said Ned.

Life was the same every day, but the sea was always different. Sometimes the waves were high as Ned's rooftop at home, and the *Adeline* rolled and pitched. Sometimes the sea was flat and calm as the pond behind his house.

Every man had his own fishing spot on deck, two lines to tend, and a barrel for the cod he caught. At the end of every day they counted each man's fish, and the captain recorded the numbers in his book. Ned would get a penny for every two fish he caught, in addition to his salary as a cook. He fished every free moment he had, so he could make more money to help out at home.

The fish were gutted and cleaned on deck, then thrown below where Ezra salted them and packed them away. It was Ned's job to scoop out the salt and bring it to Ezra. He filled the scoop to overflowing and, whenever Ezra wasn't looking, spilled a little on the floor, so it would be used up faster.

"Never known a boy more generous with salt," Ezra grumbled.

The first weeks out they caught more than one thousand fish a day. When the school had been all caught up, they heaved up the anchor and sailed off to try a new spot, where they stayed for a few weeks more.

Ned made fish chowder for supper every night. On Sundays he made donuts for breakfast and for supper he made steamed apple pudding and fried mince pies.

One night the captain ordered him to prepare a supper of boiled rice and bean soup. Ned was an old hand at bean soup, but it had been a long time since his mother had taught him how to boil rice and he didn't remember how.

Ezra came into the galley. "What are you standing around for boy? We'll be wanting supper soon."

Ned had no choice but to ask him if he knew how much rice he was supposed to measure out.

"Two quarts, at least," said Ezra and he headed back on deck.

XXXX

Ned added the rice to the water in the big boiler on the stove. While the rice began to boil, Ned tended the beans. When he looked back at the rice it was swelling and rising quickly in the boiler. In a moment it had filled the boiler and started running over the top of the stove. Ned grabbed another pot and caught what he could, but the rice kept swelling and it filled that, too. Ned ran and got another pot, and soon that was full.

Ned got every pot he could find and filled them up, and finally he filled even the water bucket. The crew was watching him and laughing, and Ned realized that Ezra had played a joke on him.

The captain came below and looked over the scene.

"Well, lad," he said, "were you planning to eat as much as fifty men this supper?"

"I'm mighty fond of rice, sir," Ned said, and everyone laughed.

After that night, Ezra would smile and say, "How about some rice for dinner?" And Ned would answer, "Sure thing, and I'll use your special recipe." While they worked below at the end of each fishing day salting the cod, Ezra told Ned tales about when he was a boy working as a cook on a schooner.

Every day Ned kept his eye on the salt, and wished he could make it disappear just by staring at it. But the salt seemed endless, and the cod seemed endless, and the days seemed endless, too. Ned knew that it was summer now, but he gave up asking what the date was. There was still salt in the last barrel. Maybe they never would head home!

At night Ned pressed his face against the bag of lavender. The lavender at home would be blooming now. The peas would be ready for picking, and the blueberries would be ripe. Mother and Nancy would be making blueberry preserves and the house would smell sweet as candy. Soon it would be his birthday and he would still be out here at sea.

Ned was surprised the next morning
that they were preparing to move the ship,
since the cod were still running strong.

"We're heading home, lad," the captain
said. "We've wet our salt."

Ned raced below. The last barrel, which
certainly had salt the day before, was empty
now.

"Ezra," Ned asked, "what happened to the
salt?"

Ezra winked. "You're needed up on deck,
boy," was all he said.

The crew was raising the mainsail and
heaving up the anchor. Ned coiled the cable
as he'd been taught. The crew was merry
and sang shanties, including Ned's favorite,
"Cape Cod Girls." He sang the verse:

"Cape Cod boys they have no sleds,
they slide down hills on codfish heads."

Adeline

It took ten days before they caught sight of land. First it was just a faint speck in the distance, then it grew to a darker smudge on the horizon.

"Cape Cod!" Ned cried.

They sailed around the tip of the Cape, into the bay. They passed Provincetown, and Truro, and finally they reached Wellfleet Harbor. The captain let Ned look through his spyglass, and he could make out the white church steeple in town.

Somewhere in the beautiful green beyond was his own house and his family waiting for him.

Ned packed all his belongings in his calico pillowcase. He had earned forty-five dollars for his job as cook and fifteen dollars extra for the three thousand fish he'd caught.

"I shall report to your mother that you were the best boy and the best cook I ever had," the captain said.

They anchored in the harbor and rowed to shore. Ned leaped out before the dinghy even touched the pier. He turned to say goodbye to the crew.

"Goodbye and happy birthday," Ezra said.

"What day is it?" Ned aked.

"July twenty-fifth," said Ezra.

"Oh, Ezra, thank you!" cried Ned. "You did that to get me home!"

"Be off with you, now," said Ezra, and he smiled.

And Ned ran off. He ran barefoot,
along the dirt road, two miles out past
town, through the fields of salt hay,
through the thickets of wild roses and
bayberry, over the hill and down into their
hollow. The lavender was in bloom and
Ned gulped great breaths of fragrant air.

Nancy was working in the garden.
She spotted him coming and cried out,
"Neddy's home!" She dashed to meet him.
He dropped his bedsack and pillowcase on
the wonderful, firm earth and caught her
up in his arms.

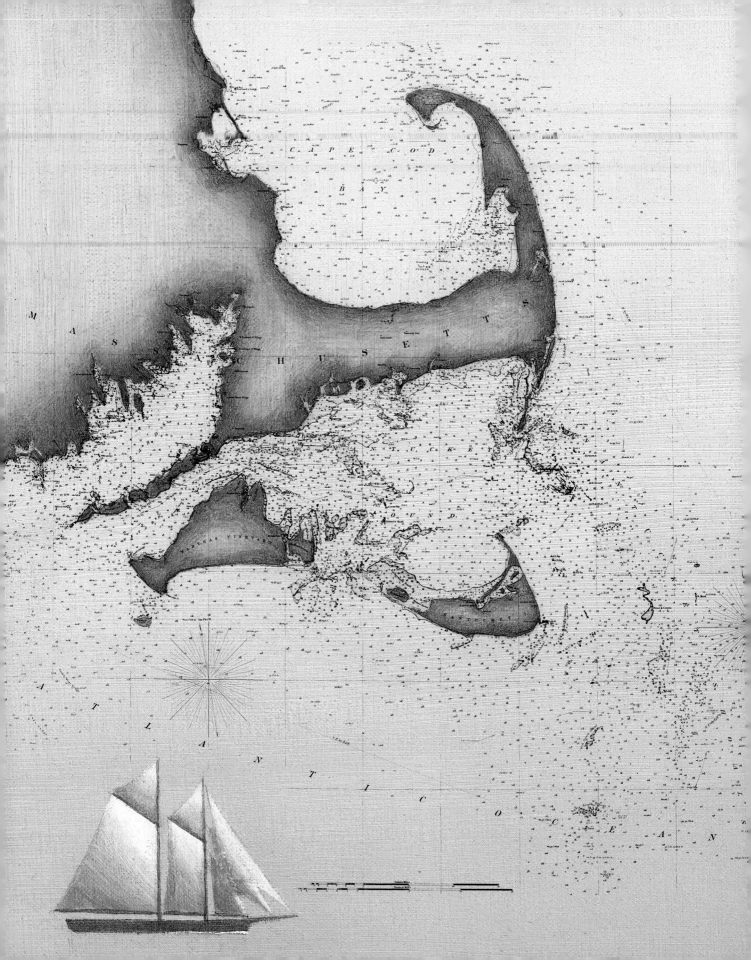

CAPE COD GIRLS

Solo — Cape Cod girls don't have no combs, Chorus — Haul a-way, haul a-way; Solo — They comb their hair with cod-fish bones, And we're bound a-way for Au - stra - lia. Chorus — So heave her up my bul-ly bul-ly boys Heave a-way, Heave a-way; Refrain — Heave her up and don't you make a noise And we're bound a-way for Au - stra - lia.

Cape Cod boys don't have no sleds, *Haul away, haul away;*
They slide down hills on codfish heads, *And we're bound away for Australia.*
Refrain

Cape Cod cats don't have no tails, *Haul away, haul away;*
They lost them all in the Northeast gales, *And we're bound away for Australia.*
Refrain

Cape Cod doctors have no pills, *Haul away, haul away;*
They give their patients codfish gills, *And we're bound away for Australia.*
Refrain

AUTHOR'S NOTE

This story is based on a narrative by Captain Joshua N. Taylor of Orleans, a town on Cape Cod, who went to sea as a cook in 1850, when he was a boy Ned's age. In the nineteenth century it was not uncommon for boys as young as eight or nine who came from large, poor families to be sent off to work on fishing and trading ships. Some, like Joshua Taylor, made the sea their lives, and rose to be captains of great sailing vessels that circled the globe. Cape Cod cemeteries are filled with tombstones commemorating the boys who never made it home at all.

Sea Yarns; Being the Reminiscences of Capt. Johsua N. Taylor, was published by the Orleans Historical Society in 1915, reprinted in 1981.